For Jessie May Allen

Bertie and the Bear
Pamela Allen

Puffin Books

Because a bear was chasing Bertie,

the Queen shouted,
'Shoo, shooo you monster YOU!'
and chased the bear.

The King took his trumpet
and blew it, BLAH! BLAH!
and chased after the Queen.

The Admiral grabbed a gong
and hit it, BONG   BONG-NG-NG
and chased after the King.

The Captain had a horn.
He blew it, OOOOOH!
and chased after the Admiral.

The General found a flute
and blew it, a-rooty toot-toot-TOOOT,
and chased after the Captain.

The Sergeant had a drum.
He banged it, BOM! BOM! BOM!
and chased after the General.

And last of all the little dog barked,
yip, yip, yip, yip, yip, yip, yip, yip,
and chased after the Sergeant.

Altogether, with the
Queen shoo shooing, and the
King BLAH   BLAHING, and the
Admiral BONG   BONGING, and the
Captain OOH   OOOHING, and the

General toot tooting, and the
Sergeant BOM BOMMING, and the
little dog yip yipping, they made

an IN-CRED-IBLE noise.

The bear stopped quite still.

He turned right around.

'All this for me?'

'Thank you,' he said.
And he bowed very low.

And because he was pleased
he stood on his head,

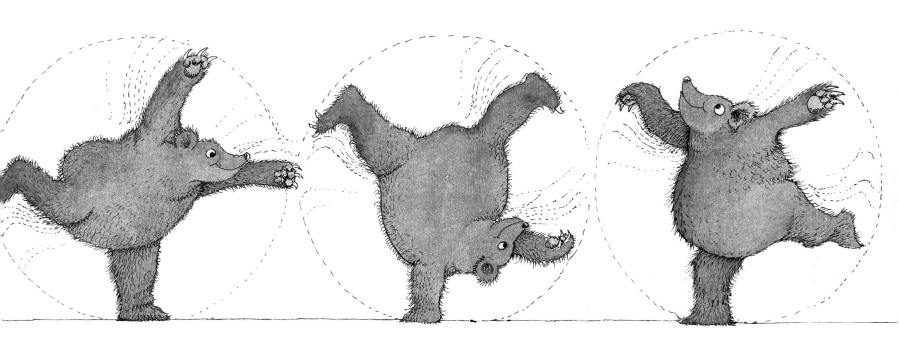

then turned a few cartwheels

and danced.

Now the bear was dancing,

Bertie danced after the bear

pom pom.